TICK TOCK & TOC

TRIPLE TROUBLE TIME

Adapted by Kris Hirschmann

© The Foundation TV Productions Limited /FunnyFlux Entertainment / EBS / CJ E&M 2014.

Published by Scholastic Inc. SCHOLASTIC and associated logos are trademarks and/or registered trademarks of Scholastic Inc.

ISBN: 978-0-545-61473-3

12 11 10 9 8 7 6 5 4 3 2 1   14 15 16 17 18 19/0
Printed in the U.S.A.   40
First printing, January 2014

SCHOLASTIC INC.

Tommy and Tallulah
want to fly their kite.

But Mother Hen needs their help.
She is sick.

She cannot watch her chicks.

The twins want to help.
They will watch the chicks
and fly their kite!

McCoggins, Lopsiloo, and
Chikidee will fly kites, too.

Battersby wants to see all four kites fly at the same time. Then he will mark his checklist.

The twins fly their kite.
But it falls down.

Uh-oh! Where are the chicks?

They take Battersby's checklist.
The chicks are trouble!

Then Pufferty arrives.

He can help them fly their kite!

The twins tie the kite
string to Pufferty.

Pufferty speeds away.

The kite lifts into the air.

Will the kites fly together?

No! The chicks peck the kite string.

The twins' kite flies away.

Tommy and Tallulah find their kite.

But where are the chicks?

They are on McCoggins's kite!

McCoggins tries to land his kite.
But his control is broken.

What a mess.

It is almost Chime Time!

And the kites did not fly together.
What will they do?

Tallulah and Tommy
have an idea.

The twins, Chikidee, and Lopsiloo fly their kites again.

They pull McCoggins's kite
to the ground.

The kites flew together!
Battersby can mark his list.

The chicks are safe.

And their mom feels better, too.

Oh, no! It's almost Chime Time!

Tommy and Tallulah race
to the clock.

The twins chime in the time!
What an adventure!